First published by Parragon in 2012
Parragon
Queen Street House
4 Queen Street
Bath BA1 1HE, UK
www.parragon.com

Edited by: Gillian Henney   Designed by: Joe Scott
Production by: Joanne Knowlson

ISBN 978-1-4454-5882-3

Printed in China

Disney
Pinocchio

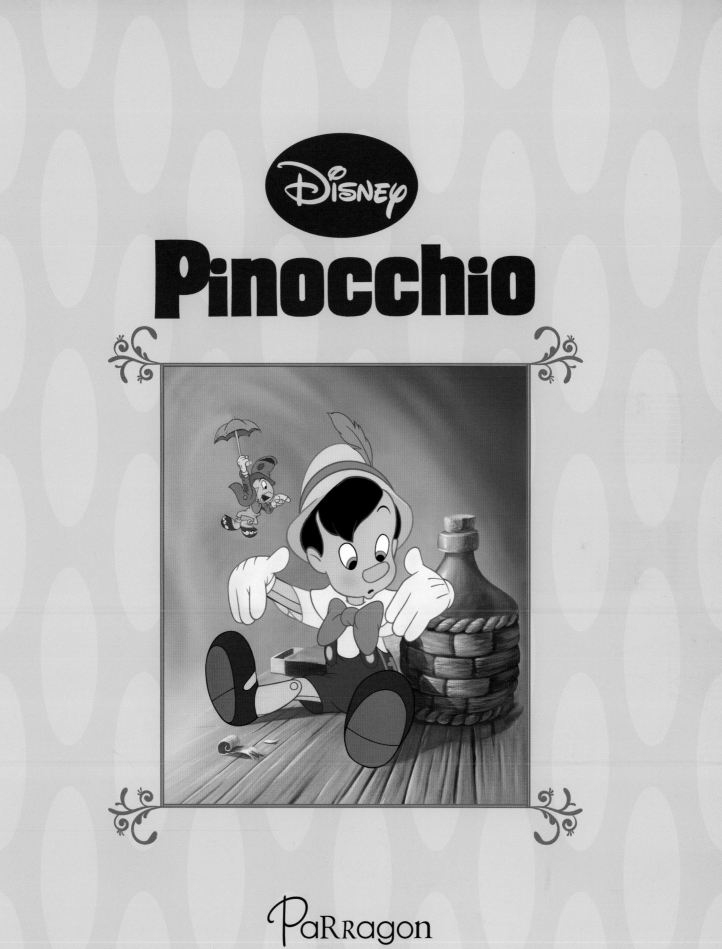

PaRragon

Bath • New York • Singapore • Hong Kong • Cologne • Delhi
Melbourne • Amsterdam • Johannesburg • Auckland • Shenzhen

Once upon a time, in a quaint little village, a beautiful wishing star shone brightly in the evening sky. A cricket named Jiminy wandered along the village streets. He spotted a lighted window, and went inside.

Jiminy Cricket looked around, amazed. He had stumbled on a woodcarver's shop full of fantastic clocks, cute little music boxes, and shelf after shelf of toys. The shop belonged to kindly old Geppetto.

Jiminy watched as Geppetto took his paintbrush, and carefully painted eyebrows and a mouth onto a small wooden puppet. Figaro, his cat, and Cleo, his goldfish, watched as he worked.

"I have just the name for you," Geppetto said when he finished. "Pinocchio!" He took Pinocchio on a little walk round his shop, balancing the puppet on his strings.

'I have just the **name** for you...

...Pinocchio!'

Later, Geppetto and Figaro climbed into bed.

Geppetto gazed out the window, looking up at the sky. "It's the Wishing Star!" he cried. Then he made a wish. As Geppetto slept, he dreamed about his wish. He had wished that Pinocchio might be a real boy.

Suddenly, a brilliant light filled Geppetto's room. It sparkled and grew into the beautiful Blue Fairy.

"Good Geppetto," the fairy said, "you deserve to have your wish come true!" She waved her magic wand over Pinocchio, saying, "Little puppet made of pine, wake! The gift is thine!"

"Am I a real boy?" Pinocchio asked.

"Not yet," the fairy explained. "First, you must prove yourself brave, truthful, and unselfish. You must learn to choose between right and wrong."

The Blue Fairy told Pinocchio that he must let his conscience be his guide. And, with a little coaxing from the Blue Fairy, Jiminy Cricket agreed to be his conscience. Then she was gone!

Geppetto, hearing strange noises, jumped out of bed. When he got to his workshop, he saw his little puppet dancing around and singing. Overjoyed, Geppetto lifted Pinocchio into the air and hugged him close.

The next morning, Geppetto walked Pinocchio outside and pointed to all the children passing by. "They are going to school," he explained. "Now that you are a little boy, you must go to school, too."

Hoping to make Geppetto proud, Pinocchio hurried off. He didn't realize that two sneaky-looking characters were watching him.

"A live puppet, with no strings!" the fox exclaimed. "We can sell him to Stromboli the puppeteer." The fox tripped Pinocchio with his cane. "I am J. Worthington Foulfellow, but my friends call me Honest John," he explained. "And this is Gideon," he added, pointing to the cat standing next to him.

Pinocchio looked up at Honest John. "I have to get to school," he explained.

Honest John convinced Pinocchio that school was a waste of time. "Come with us," he coaxed. "We'll make you a star."

Back at Geppetto's workshop, Jiminy Cricket hurried into his coat and hat, and ran out the door to follow Pinocchio to school. He saw Honest John, Gideon, and Pinocchio heading down the street—in the wrong direction!

Soon Jiminy Cricket caught up with Pinocchio and tried to change his mind. But it was too late. Honest John had convinced Pinocchio to go on stage. They were going to see Stromboli the puppeteer.

Hi-Diddle-
Dee-Dee....

Clap! Clap! Clap!

Honest John led Pinocchio right into Stromboli's greedy hands.

That night, Pinocchio made his stage debut with Jiminy Cricket in the audience. Everyone was amazed to see a singing, dancing puppet with no strings. When the show was over, the crowd applauded wildly and threw gold coins at Pinocchio's feet. Pinocchio loved all the attention—and Stromboli loved all the money the little puppet had made him!

Later that night, Pinocchio couldn't wait to get home and tell Geppetto all about his new career. When Stromboli heard Pinocchio talking about going home, he threw him in a cage and locked the door.

As Pinocchio cried and called out for Jiminy, the cricket sneaked into Stromboli's wagon. Jiminy couldn't believe his eyes when he saw Pinocchio locked in a cage.

As Jiminy was trying to free Pinocchio, the Blue Fairy appeared. When she asked Pinocchio why he hadn't gone to school, Pinocchio told so many lies that his nose grew.

Realizing what he had done wrong, Pinocchio promised that he would never lie again. The Blue Fairy agreed to give him another chance and set him free, before disappearing once more.

Haha haha haha haaa!

Jiminy and Pinocchio jumped down from the cage and ran home as fast as they could, knowing how worried Geppetto would be. He had been out all night looking for Pinocchio.

In a nearby tavern, Honest John and Gideon were meeting with a dastardly Coachman who had an evil scheme to lure boys to Pleasure Island. The Coachman promised Honest John and Gideon lots of money if they would help him find some boys.

Soon Honest John and Gideon were back on the streets, where they spotted Pinocchio. Pretending that Pinocchio looked sickly, Honest John convinced the little puppet that he needed some rest and relaxation— on Pleasure Island.

Honest John and Gideon led Pinocchio down the street. They told him all about the wonders of Pleasure Island—games, toys, candy, rides—and it was all free!

Poor Jiminy tried to catch up to them, but again it was no use.

Outside the village, Honest John turned Pinocchio over to the Coachman. Pinocchio climbed aboard a stagecoach filled with boys. The Coachman cracked his whip and off they went to Pleasure Island. The stagecoach raced through the countryside, pulled by several scared-looking donkeys.

When the boys arrived on Pleasure Island, they could hardly believe their eyes! There were fairground rides, lots of treats—and no grown-ups around to tell them what to do! The boys could be as naughty as they liked.

Pinocchio soon made friends with a boy named Lampwick.

"If my mother could see me now, she'd have a fit," he explained to Pinocchio, who was about to sample some sugary treats.

While Pinocchio was busy getting up to mischief with Lampwick, Jiminy Cricket thought it would be a good idea to explore the island. He came upon the Coachman giving orders to his men. "Shut the doors and lock them tight!"

Jiminy knew he had to find Pinocchio right away!

Jiminy saw a light in the pool hall. There he found Pinocchio and Lampwick playing pool.

"You're coming right home with me!" Jiminy cried.

Lampwick laughed. "You're taking orders from a grasshopper?" Poor Pinocchio was caught between his new friend and his conscience.

On his way back out, Jiminy saw the Coachman and his men putting donkeys in crates. "You boys will bring me a nice price." The Coachman smiled.

Jiminy realised that the donkeys were actually the boys of Pleasure Island!

Jiminy ran back to warn Pinocchio. But it was too late! Lampwick had already changed into a donkey, and was charging around in fear. Poor Pinocchio stared in horror as he sprouted his own set of donkey ears and a tail.

"Quick! We've got to get out of here!" yelled Jiminy. Pinocchio and Jiminy Cricket raced across the now-deserted island, leaving the Coachman and poor donkeys behind. They climbed up the cliff rocks and jumped into the sea.

Exhausted, the pair finally reached the shore and headed for home. But when they arrived, Geppetto was nowhere to be found.

A dove flying overhead dropped a letter for Pinocchio. The letter said that Geppetto had gone looking for Pinocchio and had been swallowed by a whale named Monstro! Pinocchio and Jiminy headed back to the sea.

At the bottom of the ocean, they began their search for Monstro. Pinocchio and Jiminy asked every fish and sea creature where to find Monstro. But no one would help them.

After searching everywhere, and after asking every fish under the sea, suddenly Pinocchio spotted Monstro, just as the monster was waking up.

Meanwhile, deep inside Monstro's belly, Geppetto was hoping for a miracle. "There isn't a fish left," he explained to poor, starving Figaro and Cleo. "If the monster doesn't wake up soon, I'm afraid we are done for!"

Suddenly Monstro started to swim. He was ready for lunch. He opened his gigantic jaws and sucked in an entire school of fish—and Pinocchio along with them!

Pinocchio and the fish swam down the whale's throat and into his giant belly. When he got there, Pinocchio found himself in the arms of a very happy Geppetto.

"We must get out of here," Pinocchio said. "But how?"

'We **must** get out of here!'

Then Pinocchio had an idea. He began chopping up furniture.

"We'll start a fire and make lots of smoke," Pinocchio said. "Then Monstro will wake up and sneeze us out!" Monstro soon felt the fire in his belly.

Inside, everyone quickly jumped onto a raft that Geppetto had built and paddled toward the whale's throat. When Monstro let out an enormous sneeze, he blew the raft out to sea.

Monstro was furious. Seeing the raft bobbing up ahead, he chased Pinocchio and Geppetto, who were holding onto the raft for dear life. Monstro reached the raft, and smashed it into pieces.

Pinocchio, holding on to Geppetto, swam with all his might. Bravely, he managed to lead Monstro into a collision with the rocks.

Pinocchio had made sure that Geppetto got safely to shore. Geppetto came to, and saw Cleo in her bowl and Figaro lying safely on the shore beside him. But when Geppetto looked around for his little son, he found him lying face-down in the water. Geppetto gently picked up Pinocchio and carried him home.

Once inside, Geppetto laid Pinocchio on his bed and knelt beside him, wishing with all his heart for Pinocchio to wake up. Suddenly the Blue Fairy appeared!

She waved her wand over Pinocchio, saying, "You have proven yourself brave, truthful, and unselfish. Now you will become a real boy!"

The lifeless wooden boy was suddenly transformed into a real live boy! Geppetto was so happy that his wish had finally come true. He wound his music boxes and they all began to dance.

What a celebration they had—the woodcarver, his son, the cat, the goldfish—and a wise cricket named Jiminy!